The Curse of The First-Born Daughter

By Noni Munro-Rogers

Published by Steve Munro
Printed in Australia by Lightning Source Australia Pty Ltd.

Paperback ISBN: 978-0-6483418-0-2

A catalogue record for this book is available from the National Library of Australia

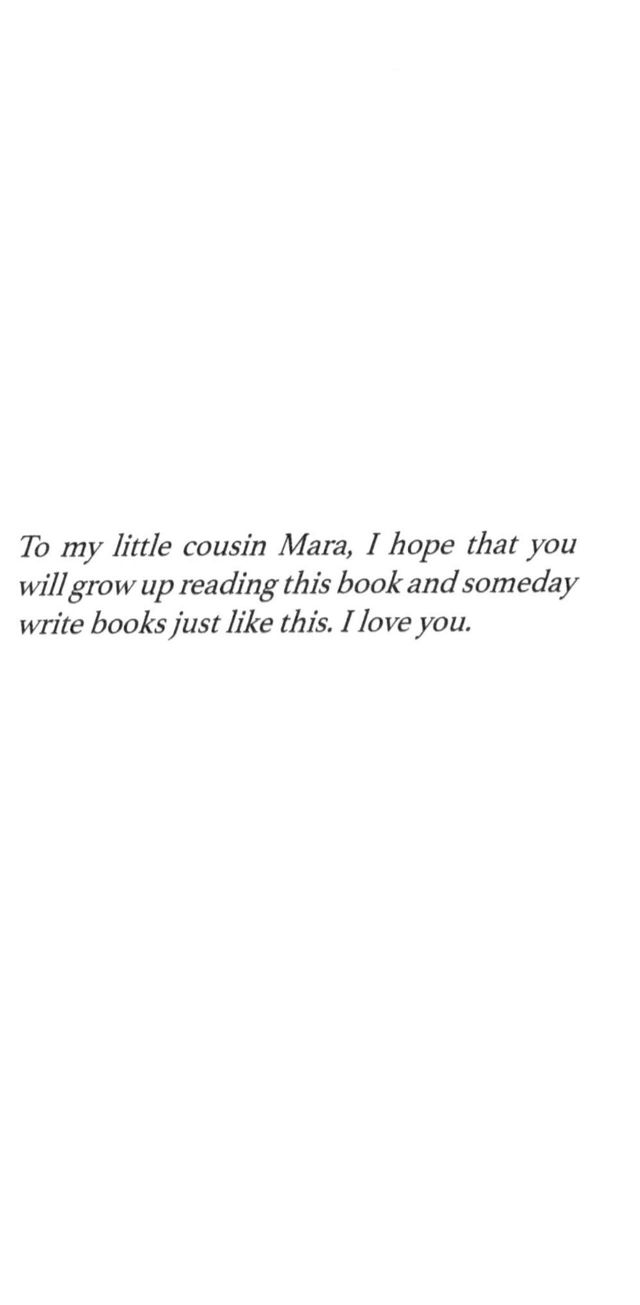

To my little cousin Mara, I hope that you will grow up reading this book and someday write books just like this. I love you.

❖ I ❖

Balls had always bored me. I didn't care if the ball was for a celebrated politician or duke, or if it was a seasonal dance. The concept of dressing up and learning to dance just to impress other self-righteous, pompous, rich friends and family never made much sense to me.

Although, not much in my life did. My life was full of dancing lessons, fittings for the constant stream of fancy ball gowns and lacy dresses for my already overflowing closet, diets and the constant criticism of my all too expectant aunties and cousins. With their perfect waists and polite manners, I could hardly fit in with their light conversation of husbands and fashion. And as for the balls, I was now having one – to my complete and utter horror – thrown for me!

My 18th birthday. My coming of age was now only a couple days away, and my mother and father wanted it to be perfect. Coming from a respected family, the guests on the list were mostly dukes and duchesses who thought they were too good for anyone else. People I barely knew and didn't care for.

My friends were of course invited. All three of them. They were the only people who shared my opinion of balls and dresses and the expectations of all the ladies around me. Although that could be because two of them were boys, Percival and Albus. The other was a girl, Agnes, who agreed with me that dresses were for girls who were happy to sit around all day and sew by the fire.

And that was not us.

We four would venture into the woods on quiet afternoons to our secret spot near a beautiful pond. There, we would talk and rant about the "perfect" lives we had.

I learnt how to hunt and fish there, things that I preferred to lace-work and sewing. The one thing that I did enjoy that was a tiny bit ladylike was reading. I could read for-ever. I had bookshelves full of every genre, every book you could ever hope of finding was right there, in my house – for we had a library so grand and beautiful it was fit for a king; and it sort of was.

My family were only one step down from royalty and owned the thousands of hectares that surrounded our manor, which was set near two villages and dense woodlands.

That library was in fact where half of the festivities for my birthday would be held. The massive bookcases had been heaved to the sides of the room, and tables and chairs and decorations of all sorts were being erected all around. It all looked far too fancy for my taste. The library was the only room big enough, aside from the ballroom itself, to hold so many people – and since my love of reading was well known, apparently that made it a fitting scene for a feast of all the food you could ever dream of.

However, I didn't think so. The library was one of my only refuges from the hectic preparations that I wanted no part of. Now, my quiet place had been infiltrated by a flurry of servants and maids, cleaning and moving furniture and placing tables. My 18th was only 3 days away, and I was dreading every second that got me closer to that day.

My Mother and Father, whom I loved dearly but occasionally got rather sick of, were over their heads with excitement. They had been planning this event for months, and now that the day had nearly arrived, they were beside themselves with the idea of their eldest daughter finally becoming a responsible adult. Of course, I had no intention of becoming like my parents. No way would I ever be like them. I would try as hard as possible to be fair and not waste away my days chatting and sewing. Although that might be, because one month after my 18th, I was to be engaged to one the snobbiest, most controlling person I have ever met. Zachariah was his name. In fact, he was second only to the man who picked him out for me – my grandfather.

My grandfather was a horrible person, completely obsessed with status, very manipulative and easily bought for any sum of money over 10,000 pounds. He had an old-fashioned way of seeing things and was religious and ridiculously superstitious. No-one in our community was more superstitious than him. I mean come on, it's the 1700s, shouldn't we start thinking differently?

As I drifted off to sleep that night, my

thoughts came back to my engagement. Did I want to get married? Was this really the life my parents thought was best for me? I certainly didn't think so. In fact, the more I thought about it, the more I started to think a life on the run would be pretty enticing. Maybe I could pose as a farmer's daughter and lay in the sun all day and read. That was the life that I wanted, away from the responsibilities of being a duke's daughter. I wasn't sure I ever wanted to marry and have kids. I wanted to be free and unattached. Maybe my friends would come too...?

I'm walking through the forest, late at night. I walk past a tree that looks different to all the oaks and birches that crowd the forest. A Rowan tree. It stands tall and proud. The moon has leached all the colour from the landscape but I can imagine the berries in clumps around the branches. I know in daylight they make the tree look like it's exploding with the most amazing red colour. Suddenly the berries start to turn red, even though everything else is still dark. Confused, I reached out to touch a berry. It's only then I realise they aren't berries, they are eyes.

❖ 2 ❖

The dreaded day had arrived. My "big day" as many were calling it. I spent the morning in a blur of fittings for my ridiculously extravagant dress, which had so many frills and bows it took me a couple minutes to work out how on earth I was going to get it on. Of course, I had the help of my maids. There were too many of them, curling my hair, tightening my corset, adding makeup to my already caked face. It was exhausting.

By the time I made it to the evening, I had no idea how I would last until late into the night. I just wanted to flop onto my bed and sleep for days. But, duty called, and I was summoned to the ball room, ready to make my all too grand entrance.

As I made my way down our winding flights of stairs, I could feel the eyes of everyone I passed boring into me. I wasn't sure how I felt about that. I quite liked being the centre of attention, but not in this way. I got to the entrance to the ball and my father was waiting for me.

"Hello Father, you look lovely."

He was dressed in a blue overcoat and ruffled shirt and had on a white wig and a lovely silk top hat. He really did look handsome, I thought. I loved my father. He could be controlling and self-absorbed at times, but he really did think that this life was best for me, even if it wasn't.

"Winona where have you been?" he asked briskly. "You should've been here 20 minutes ago."

"Sorry, sorry," I replied.

The doors opened and my heartrate quickened as hundreds of eyes turned towards me and didn't look away. I took a shaky step into the room and everyone started clapping, although I had no idea why. I looked around, wondering who they could possibly be clapping for, then I realised: they were clapping for me! I felt a smile creep onto my face and tried to smother it with a gloved hand.

I failed and ended up not bothering. I was beaming. All of this for me? Maybe life here wasn't so bad. Sure, I would have preferred a little more freedom but the love put into all this was very clear.

As the night continued, people came up to me one by one, or in pairs or small groups, congratulating me on making it to adulthood and asking questions like, "have you found a husband yet?" and statements like, "you really should pull up your bust-line, it's showing too much."

My grandfather came up to me and started talking about my wedding in a month's time. He was a little drunk, but sober enough to make me try to get away as soon as possible.

My encounter with Grandfather, mixed with all the commotion, was all a little too much for me to handle, so I snuck out for a bit and went to the roof. How I managed to climb onto the roof in all the jewellery and clothing I had on was a complete mystery to me. But I made it and once up there, I lay on the tiles and looked up at the sky. It was a clear night and we were far enough away from the light and smog of London that I could see millions of stars. They really were beautiful, once you got over the whole cold light and vastness of the universe, which if you thought about it too much, could be really frightening.

Time wore on and I decided people were probably starting to realise I had left the party. I stood up, balanced myself on the sloping roof and brushed off my dress, hoping no one would notice the inevitable stain on my bottom. I was about to shimmy down the piping when my shoe slipped. I started sliding uncontrollably down the remaining part of the roof.

Damn it all! I thought, then mentally scolded myself for swearing.

All the while the roof was disappearing far too quickly and just as I was about to go over the edge, I managed to catch onto an eave that held no purpose on our roof whatsoever. I was glad for it at that moment and caught myself before I slipped any farther. But now my legs were dangling off the roof and if anyone had looked up, they would have been alarmed to see a girl's underwear dangling four stories above them. I mustered all my strength and pulled myself back onto the roof.

Breathing a sigh of relief, I got down as fast and safely as I could. I wouldn't be going up there anytime soon. Flustered, I hurried back inside, certain people would now be wondering where I was. I was correct. As soon as I had set foot in the room, my mother rushed up to me, my little sister in tow.

"Nona darling, where on earth have you been? You can't just leave your own party! It's not polite. Now go and talk to someone respected, maybe you could learn something from them."

I brushed my mother's suggestion aside. "No thank you, I think I'll go and find Percy and Albus."

She sighed. "Okay, but don't get into any more trouble please."

She pinched my cheek a little too hard and bustled off, intent on handing my younger sister Jessamine onto someone else so she could drink with her friends and gossip about the town ladies. I sat down for a bit, thinking over everything that had just happened. I nearly died, I realised. If that eave hadn't been there, I would've plummeted 50 feet to the ground below, breaking my neck and having my insides become my outsides.

I decided to brush it off, and never let it happen again. Those damn shoes, I thought. Why is Mother so obsessed with me wearing shoes with such little grip?

The dinner bell was called and everyone, all 400 dukes, duchesses, princes and princesses, people I barely knew, filed into the library and sat at their assigned tables. I was on a table with my mother, father and three best friends. Agnes wasn't from a particularly wealthy family, so she was often scorned by the clothes she wore and how she spoke. Today though, she had borrowed a dress of mine. I said she could keep it but she politely declined.

"No thank you. I wouldn't want to wreck something like this. And please, do you really think I would wear it on any other day than today?"

She wore only a little makeup, highlighting the lovely features of her face. She spoke with a politeness I only heard when she was around my parents and others thought her to be the daughter of some wealthy duke or politician. Albus and Percival, coming from wealthy families, had been brought up the same way I had. Clean clothes are key, always use the right cutlery for the right meal, and always be polite to everyone outside your family.

They were very practiced and a lot more relaxed than Agnes was, although she was starting to get the feel of the whole cutlery thing. I feel sure that later, when we were talking privately in my bedroom, she would make a comment about the atrocious amount of cutlery needed for a full banquet.

"Who uses all those spoons? What are half of them even for? Picking up caviar, one by one?"

It was always funny the way she regarded the life I lived, as if it were a foreign language or place.

Finally, it all ended and I bid farewell to the last of our guests. Only Agnes, Percival and Albus stayed, and they made it clear they were staying the night. I dumped them all into separate rooms and trudged back to mine.

It was nearly three o'clock in the morning.

I stood in a half-asleep stupor as my maids undressed me and put my nightclothes on. I fell into bed, but even though I was exhausted, sleep wouldn't come. I lay awake, thinking about the dream I'd had a couple of nights ago, with Rowan trees and red eyes, and wondered what it meant...

My thoughts stopped there and I rolled into a deep, dreamless sleep.

❖ 3 ❖

I awoke the next morning – or afternoon I soon found out – feeling rather peculiar. I suspected it was just the aftermath of last night's events. Partying early into the morning and drinking more champagne than I was used to was bound to take its toll on my exhausted body.

It wasn't just that though, something else seemed quite off. I couldn't put my finger on it so I shook it off and lay in bed, relishing the quietness of a sleeping house.

Unfortunately, that peace and quiet didn't last long as my eight-year-old brother came bounding into my room, shouting obscenities that made my head implode. As soon as he entered, my head started pounding. This was more than just a headache, but I tried to push the pain aside.

"Hello Gussie, how are you today?"

He didn't reply but jumped onto my bed and crawled under the covers with me.

Augustus, Gussie to me, was my youngest sibling. He and Jessamine, my eleven-year-old sister, often played together. Although they were different genders, they managed to work their way around the different expectations for them. Often their play lead to dirt, which lead to Mother having small hissy fits and immediately calling for a maid.

"Nona, Nona!" Gussie cried, 'I stayed up 'til eleven o'clock last night! I'm as grown up as you are!"

"Yes, you did stay up late. Are you tired now?"

"Not at all," he declared proudly, although I could see that in a couple of hours he would become cranky and need to sleep.

He left to find Jess soon after, obviously bored with me. I snuggled back into my duvet, hoping to maybe get a couple more hours of sleep. But no, not five minutes after Gus had left, the door cracked open again and my three best friends waltzed in.

"Top of the morning, isn't it?" Percy said loudly. Then he rethought that, "no actually, it's the afternoon, isn't it?"

Agnes and Albus laughed and climbed onto the bed. The pounding in my head increased and I could barely keep a straight face. Percival joined them and we talked about last night's events.

"I heard that Lady Genevieve and Duke Zachariah are to be married next week," said Agnes.

"Pffft, who cares about that? Anybody up to a walk in the woods?" Albus replied. How he had any energy to go for a walk was beyond me. Apparently though, I was the only one feeling bad. The others jumped up and after I explained I had a dreadful headache, they went out and I didn't hear from them for the rest of the afternoon.

Back in peace and quiet, my headache lessened and the pounding stopped. But something was very wrong. I had a sore throat, and not just the type you get from a cold. This was much, much worse, and I didn't have any other symptoms of a cold.

I got up and walked over to the window. Afternoon sunlight was streaming in through the window in a lovely golden colour. Hoping to catch some of the warmth that it gave off, I lay on the floor in a patch of sun.

I felt a tingling sensation all over my body, and all of a sudden my skin felt as if someone was running hot coals up and down it. It was excruciating and I stumbled back into the shadows.

What is wrong with me?

I decided a cold bath would help me, so I called in my personal handmaiden, Agatha, to run me a cool bath. She didn't question me, although I can imagine the thoughts running through her head. A cool bath? At this time of day? Dearie me, she is acting weird.

I slipped into the cool waters of the bath and my skin fizzled. Alarmed, I got ready to jump out, but found that it was the only way to cool my burnt skin. Agatha looked at me in a weird way again but didn't question it.

"That'll be all. Thank you, Agatha,"

"Yes ma'am," she curtsied and exited the room quickly.

Again, in the quiet, I wondered what had been happening to me today. Burning throat, burning skin, pounding noises in my ears. It was almost as if I was allergic to sunlight. Maybe I was. But what about the pounding head? It had intensified when Gus and my friends had come in, and receded when they had left. It was like I could hear their heartbeats. But no, that couldn't be it. The most logical explanation for all this was I'd had too much to drink last night and stayed up way too late. Heartbeats, I scoffed. Of course, I wasn't hearing heartbeats.

But as much as I tried to brush it off, I had a nagging feeling at the back of my mind that something was seriously wrong with me.

That night, I was called down to dinner. Although I felt I was not well enough to go, duty called, and I had to. By duty, I mean Mother storming up the stairs and lecturing me about politeness. I sighed as she helped me dress into my evening attire and followed her down. As I entered the dining room, my head exploded. I gave a small scream and folded in on myself, holding my head and willing for it to go away. It didn't and when Father came up to me, wondering what on earth was happening to his daughter, it intensified. I had to leave. I gave the dining room one last sweeping look before Agatha helped me back to my bedroom. Father looked bewildered, Mother, slightly scared. Jessamine was holding Gussie, who looked like he was about to cry, and my friends were horrified. They got up to try to follow me but Mother told them to sit down, Agatha would take care of this.

Back up in my room, in a hot bath that Agatha had prepared for me, my head calmed down. I sighed with relief and sunk under the water, completely covering myself in the warm, sweet smelling bubbly water. I thought back to what had just happened. It was as if, for one fleeting moment, I had lost control; if I hadn't regained it, I had a horrible feeling that I wouldn't be where I was right now.

That night, I went to bed sure that there was something going on. I had tried to brush my hair with my metal hairbrush and again I had been burnt. All these random things happening! It was starting to freak me out, and I had even started thinking of the supernatural.

But even that didn't make sense to me. Were-wolves got burnt by silver, but didn't get burnt in the sunlight, witches had a weird reaction to fire. But nothing had ever happened like this before. As far as I knew. But then, there was no such things as witches and werewolves. Once in a while there was an old hag who claimed she had the power of her ancestors, but who really believed that? I decided I would find out in the morning.

❖ 4 ❖

I didn't make it to the morning. I awoke in the middle of the night, throat worse than ever. In a daze, I walked to my door and it was as if a string was tugging at me through my stomach. Before I realised what I was doing, I had left my house and walked deep into the woods. The invisible string stopped tugging at me and I came to a halt in front of a deer carcass that could've only been a day or two old. Without thinking, I dropped to my knees and plunged my teeth into the carcass, drinking and drinking until I had completely drained the deer of blood.

Only then did I realise what I had done.

Horrified, I lifted my fingers to my mouth, wondering how I had even punctured the deer's hide, and I found that two of my front teeth had grown, forming two very sharp fangs. I gave a small scream and stumbled back to the house.

What was I?

I stayed in my room for a couple of days, claiming to have a horrific headache and refusing help. I had decided that I would never do that again, I'd rather die. I only lasted a few days though, the household was suspicious and worried and whenever Agatha brought food, I turned it down. I was hungry, but eating food no longer brought me the pleasure it once had.

As much as I tried to fight it, the burning was worse than before and finally I succumbed. I snuck down to the pantry and found a fox hanging from the roof. The bounty of Father's earlier hunting party, no doubt. I checked to make sure no one was around and ran over to it. I drank and drank, relieved that the pain was lessening. I slowed down now, and took my time.

No one would come in here at this time of day, I told myself.

But, just as I thought that, someone came in through the door. I looked up in alarm, blood dripping down my face, and saw our cook Nora staring at me with a terrified look on her face.

"DEMON!" she screamed. "DEMON!"

I'd never heard anyone be so loud. Father came rushing in. He looked at me and whispered something; it sounded like, "Father warned me of this."

A terrible look came across his face as he grabbed a kitchen knife and advanced towards me. I stepped backwards.

What had my grandfather warned him about? Did it have something to do with what was happening to me?

The world came back into focus when suddenly my father came at me, thrusting the knife deep into my stomach.

I gasped and looked into his eyes.

Tears were threatening to spill over onto his face as he stepped back. "I'm sorry," he whispered, and he came at me again.

I was too shocked to move, but it didn't hurt for some reason. Maybe I was too worked up to feel anything? I stood there while he lunged at me. Finally, I kicked into gear, adrenaline surging through me and I sprinted out the side door. Although blood was pouring out of my stomach, I didn't stop until I was far, far away from my house. A house I would never go back to, I thought sadly.

By now I was deep into the forest and my stab wound had really started hurting, I wondered how on earth I was going to survive something like that.

I curled up in a nearby cave and sobbed. I cried and cried. Thinking about the monster I had become and what I was scared I could do, what I probably would do, given the chance. Would I lose control around humans? Would I want to sink my fangs into their necks and drink their warm, alive blood? Would I ever have a family again? I didn't think so, I had been thrown out for good.

❖ 5 ❖

The next couple of days were all a blur. I found out some interesting things about my new situation. Father had placed watchmen all around the premises of my ex-home. And my stab wound healed up the next day! I didn't put anything on it, but when I woke up it had completely gone. On about the third night of being cast out, I also discovered that I couldn't be in the sunlight. If I was, I got severe burns all along my arms. But these healed up straight away, of course.

Soon I ventured into the nearby town of Kamdyn to look for food and information. I snuck into the local butchers and found a freshly slain pig in the ice pantry. It was closed so I had to break in.

Next I went to the library, where I found several books on my situation. There wasn't much, only one or two books, but I decided that I had become something people had only ever heard of, never actually seen. A vampire. Vampirism was a curse, a curse that had not existed until around the time I had been born. The books told me that when the cursed person had a near death experience, it would trigger this unholy being inside of you and eventually, it would burst out. You'd be allergic to sunlight, have incredible senses and reflexes, and if you touched metal your hand would burn to the bone. And of course there was the need to drink blood.

I found that although my body still needed food and water, they would become necessities rather than pleasures.

There were, of course, perks to being what I had become. I was now ten times faster than I had been, I could hear someone's heartbeat from hundreds of feet away, and I could smell the sweat and fear of everyone in the village.

It saddened me to think that I was the cause of their terror. Father had obviously told everyone that there had been a demon in his household. But I was also angry, as this was hardly my fault.

I heard talk of a witch and her apprentice. At least, people believed this woman to be a witch, though who knew if she really was?

But since there was no such thing as vampires until now, and barely anybody had heard of them, I'd decided to give this witch thing a shot. Maybe witches were true after all. I thought if they could help me come to terms with my new self, I'd feel a lot better about the whole "being thrown out of home right after my eighteenth birthday" thing. And so it began, my search for these two people who could possibly help me.

I searched for days on end but had no luck. Eventually I made my way to London. I had run all the way there, and surprisingly had not tired at all. As I prowled the streets at night, the smells of London intoxicated me, the smog and the dirt now ten times worse than the last time I had been in London with my mother. Aside from the smell, I quite enjoyed London, all the different varieties of people, and their blood.

But no, I told myself. I would not drink the blood of humans. I would never drink the blood of a human, that had become my absolute rule.

One particularly cloudy night, I was walking back to the little hideout I had found for when the daytime came. I found I no longer needed much sleep so I entertained myself during the day by drawing pictures with bits of charcoal on the walls around me.

Out of the blue, I got the feeling someone was following me, I turned around and saw nothing but I had been certain that I had heard footsteps echoing on the bricks. I turned a corner and hid behind a rather smelly dumpster and waited to see who my pursuer was. Someone rounded the corner and I pounced, knocking them down. We struggled for a bit and eventually I ended up on top of whoever I was fighting against.

Wow, when did I get so good at fighting? Another perk of being a vampire, I suppose.

I finally got a good look at my attacker, I say he had shoulder length dark blond hair, and was insanely good looking. He had a surprised look on his face, possibly wondering how a girl could fight that well. The surprise only made him more beautiful.

How could one person be that good looking? I wondered.

"Um. What?" he said.

Oops. Apparently, I'd wondered aloud.

"Nothing," I said, and rolled off him.

He got up and brushed himself off. He obviously had no intention of helping me to get up. How ungentlemanly of him. Bothered, I got up and stood in front of him. He towered above me. He must have been 6 foot 4 leaving me, standing at an infuriating 5 foot one, to crane my neck to look at him.

"Who are you?" I asked rudely. If he could be impolite, so could I.

"The name's Ambrose. I work for the witch Letitia. You heard of me?"

His accent was rather hard to understand, it had a slight Irish lilt to it, I thought. Very different from the posh King's English I was used to.

I stared. This was the guy I had been looking for? I was disappointed. Couldn't whoever was going to help me be even the slightest bit more... polite?

I sighed. I guess I was going to have to get used to it. As a blood-sucking monster, I doubted many people would be very friendly towards me now.

"Have you been following me?" I asked, although I was almost certain of the answer.

"That I have been," he said. His choice of words infuriated me. I don't know why, but something about him set me off. I'd only just met this guy and already he'd annoyed me several times.

"Why have you been following me? There's been a lot of talk going around the magic folk about you recently. The first ever recorded vampire in history, you should feel special."

"Hardly," I grumbled.

He chuckled. "Come with me. Letitia wants to meet you."

I followed him out of the alleyway, aware that the sun would soon be rising but I was curious enough to meet this Letitia that I decided to risk it. We walked and we walked, all through the back alleyways of London.

I had just started wondering if he actually knew where he was going when we came to a small shop. The sign on the front read:

Thwaites and Reed
Antique clocks since 1642

I doubted it was still a clock shop, and assumed it was just to cover up on what was really going on inside. I was correct. Inside, piles of old books, manuscripts and jars of who knows what filled up the whole room. Lining the walls were shelves stacked with more books and jars. I went over to take a closer look at one of the jars and found the hazy eyes of a toad staring right back at me. I shuddered and returned to Ambrose's side.

"Do you really live here?" I supressed another shudder at the thought of having to spend the night here with all the jarred eyeballs and hearts. Ugh. I may now be a vampire but even I had limits. And pickled hearts and jellied eyes were far beyond that limit. I mean, I was living in an abandoned building, so I couldn't really say much. But at least it was relatively clean. For an old building, that is.

"Right now? No, I live in the Convent."

There was an awkward silence and I was wondering what we were actually doing here when an old lady shuffled in. Her face was covered in wrinkles and a long, purple scar ran down the left side of her face, blinding one eye and turning her lips into grotesque lumps.

I swallowed a shudder and forced myself to look directly into her eye. "My name is Winona Hosking, and I've come to ask for your help. I believe I have become something called a 'vampire'. Have you heard of this condition?"

"I wondered when I'd see you again," the woman said. Her voice was raspy, as if she had swallowed decades of sand and grit. She probably had.

"But I've never met you before," I said, intrigued.

"Yes, that is quite right. You've never met me. But I've met you. It was 18 years ago, you were still in your Mother's stomach when I paid a visit. I found out that she was having a daughter, and I had to fulfil my end of a deal that I made with your grandfather years and years ago."

I immediately became suspicious. My grandfather could've made any number of deals that gave him wealth and made everyone around him suffer.

"What was that deal?" I asked, afraid of what I might hear.

"In turn for years and years of wealth and fortune, your grandfather agreed for the first-born girl in his family line to be born with the curse of bad luck. Unfortunately for you, the curse spiralled out of my control and I had to let it go. Since I no longer had a grip on it, it grew and exploded into the curse that you now rest with. Yes, you are the first ever vampire. You are a twist of nature, a break in the universe. You shall live for eternity unless you stay in the sunlight too long, in which case you will turn to ash. And be warned, there is only one other way to kill you, a much faster way. The stake of a Rowan tree. Should you be stabbed directly in the heart by one of these it will be a quick but painful death. But I wouldn't worry too much, I have only ever seen one of them made. You are going to have a long and lonely life, m'lady," she grinned at my shock and discomfort. "But my dear, it's not all bad. You have the power to bring back the dying. One small bite and they will come back as a vampire. Like you."

And with that, the old lady shuffled back out of the room.

I sat down on the nearest seat I could find, a crate filled with who knows what. I feared I would faint if I stayed standing any longer. I felt betrayed, and for good reason too. My grandfather, my blood, had traded my life for his good fortune?

"Are you okay?"

I jumped. I'd forgotten that Ambrose was still with me. "No, I am not alright at all. These past couple of days I've nearly died several times, drunk the blood of animals, run for days on end to get here, only to find out when I get here that my selfish grandfather betrayed me before I was even born. And I'm still coming to terms with all that, so no, I am not alright."

"I'm very sorry," was all he said as he sat down beside me.

When night fell, Ambrose led me back out of the shop and we walked in silence for a while. I didn't have any idea which direction my hideout was and I had no idea if we were going the right way. We turned a corner, and I tensed. Up ahead was the last person I wanted to see.

My grandfather was leaning against the brick wall of the factory we had just walked around. He had his hands in his pockets and a long cigar in his mouth.

Although this was his typical position, I could sense something was wrong. Slowly, I approached him, wondering if he'd seen me.

❖ 6 ❖

"Grandfather?" I asked. I was unsure if he was actually awake, or just in a dream faze. It sometimes happened with old people.

He started and looked at me. Yes, there was definitely an evil glint in his eye.

Cautiously, I took several steps back. He lunged at me, pulling something long and white out of his coat pocket. For some reason, I immediately recognised it, although I have no clue how.

It was the Rowan wood stake that the witch had mentioned only hours earlier.

Ambrose and I kicked into action at the same time, Ambrose running towards Grandfather, and me sprinting in the opposite direction. I skidded to a halt and turned around to see Ambrose holding his hands out towards my Grandfather.

"AMBROSE!" I yelled. "WHAT IN THE NAME OF GOD ARE YOU DOING?!"

"ENTRANCING YOUR GRANDFATHER," he yelled back.

It was only then that I realised that the crazy, charging old man had turned into a docile puppy. His eyes had glazed over and he was swaying from side to side. I wondered if he would topple over. Slowly, I walked forwards and saw he was muttering something. It looked like Ambrose's grip on the entrancement was starting to loosen and second by second, my grandfather was getting more and more enraged.

I got close enough to hear what he was muttering.

"I must kill you. If anyone finds out my granddaughter is cursed, it will be the end of me. Please, I've got to kill you."

I stepped back, shocked that he could be so evil as to want to kill his own granddaughter. Just then, Ambrose completely lost control over him. My grandfather lunged towards me, I dodged to the left and kicked behind his knees, making his leg collapse. Despite the horror of being attacked by my own grandfather, I was really enjoying my new skills. He regained his posture and turned around again, ready for another attempt. I dodged him and dodged him, I now had such good reflexes. I had never expected to be able to dodge around Grandfather so many times. This went on for ages and ages, Grandfather snarling obscenities at me, and me shouting them back while dodging his blows.

He did get a couple of good hits on me though, and I was soon covered in scratches that were excruciatingly painful and bleeding all over the place. Apparently, the only thing that could actually give me a bad wound was the stake he was holding in his hand. Eventually, I saw he was beginning to tire, and I started throwing harder punches and more forceful kicks. I, of course, hadn't tired at all, and I assumed that I wouldn't have, had this ordeal continued.

But it all stopped when I cornered Grandfather, punched him and he hit his head on the brick wall behind him. He lost consciousness and fell to the ground.

I stepped back and looked at my grandfather, lying there on a London street. Ambrose came up behind me and I jumped. I had forgotten he had been there.

Ambrose hadn't joined in the fight, obviously believing that I was doing fine on my own. Which I was, but it would've been a whole lot faster if he had just magicked my grandfather to sleep or something. Now the sun was almost rising and I had nowhere to go.

I was really starting to panic, and looked over at Ambrose for help. He just shrugged. Ugh, why was he so frustrating? And it doesn't help that he was good looking, either. He was infuriatingly good looking. And no one that upsetting should be allowed to have such a perfect body. Shaking my head to make myself concentrate, I looked at him. "What do we do with him?"

"Just leave him there. He'll wake up. Eventually."

❖ **7** ❖

And so, we left my grandfather lying in a dark alleyway where hopefully no one would find him before he woke up.

We raced back to my hideout, which turned out to be only a couple of blocks away. I made it just in time, as my skin had started to tingle as the sun rose.

We sat in the shadows of my building and talked. Ambrose actually wasn't all bad, I discovered. We talked about my life, I told him that I had come from a very wealthy family but had always wanted to get away from it all. And in return, he told me that he had never had a family. Letitia had found him when he was around four in a forest near a city, although he didn't know which one. He didn't know exactly how old he had been, and he didn't have a birthday. All he had were a few memories. Flashes of red hair and another little child that smelled of baby.

"Everybody has a birthday," I said, surprised.

"Not me," he said sadly. 'I don't even know what year I was born in."

He looked to be about two years older than me, maybe twenty? I decided that, even though he annoyed me at times, I would try to cheer him up.

"Well, you can share my birthday if you want, or maybe we can make one up for you?"

It sounded rather childish, as if I was talking to a five-year-old, but he seemed to like the idea so we came up with a birthday for him. The 8th of April, a couple of months before mine. My birthday was the 31st of July. Being at the end of the month was considered rarer than any other date of the month. But only by a little, and not by many.

By the time the sun set, we had come up with a plan. Ambrose decided that he was coming with me, to help find other witches or sorcerers who might know more about what I had become.

I asked why he was coming and he had simply answered, "My adoptive mother put the curse on you, so it is my duty to help you with it."

But I reckoned there was more to it than meets the eye. I was starting to like him more and more. One day, I suspected, it might turn into something completely different. Maybe he felt the same? I certainly hoped so. We would travel by night train to the edge of Liverpool, where we would walk to the nearby forest. Ambrose had heard that a powerful sorcerer lived here. Whether he knew anything about vampires, Ambrose didn't know, but it was worth a try. After we had visited the sorcerer, if he had information, we would stay longer. But if not, we would walk through the forest to a little hunting cabin that Ambrose knew of. He had spent a bit of time in the forests surrounding Liverpool when he was little. There, we would stay and work out what to do after that.

I had become excited at the thought of running away, especially with someone that I liked. The feeling of freeness would come to me and I hoped that I would be happy. Happier than I was back at home, happier than I've ever been. And right now, despite all that was happening, I was beginning to feel that sense of happiness. I would miss my best friends, I wondered what they thought of me now, would they be horrified by the story that my father had surely told them? Or would they not believe him and are they wondering where I am? Do they miss me? I didn't miss Mother and Father at all, and my recent encounter with Grandfather made me want to get away as soon as possible.

But I missed my brother and sister dearly. Jessie probably believed what my father told her. She worshipped him and would do anything he asked of her. But Gussie? I hoped that he wouldn't think bad of me. I believed that he was too young to come to terms with what had happened. To him, his older sister, whom he loved a lot, had disappeared without a trace, and for some reason no one in the household would speak her name. I felt terrible for that. I would miss him a lot, more than anybody else. But much as I hated to admit it, it was possibly for the better that he didn't grow up with someone like me around.

As our plan grew, so did my hopes. I had become certain that we would find someone who knew something about all of this. What a vampire could and couldn't do, because god only knows how long it would take me to figure it out alone. A couple of centuries, perhaps?

I decided to try to send a letter to my friends. I wouldn't bother sending one to my family –surely, they would toss it into the fire upon seeing who it was from. But I wouldn't be sending Agnes, Albus and Percival an ordinary letter. Ambrose said he knew a tricky spell to send letters directly from the sender to the receiver without any detours. I didn't doubt Ambrose's ability for magic, but I was just still getting used to it. I believed one day his magic will help us immensely – in fact, I had a feeling that that day would be soon.

Later that night I sat on the floor, with a couple of pieces of paper and a candle that Ambrose had given me.

I wrote:

To my best friends Agnes, Albus and Percy,

My friends, I apologise for my abrupt disappearance, but after what happened, I got the feeling that I was no longer wanted in that household. I do so hope that you don't all hate me now. I do understand if you believe all that my father says, I would too, but if you can find it in yourselves to believe that I am not all evil, I like to believe that I am not even the slightest bit, although I know I am, drinking the blood of animals isn't exactly good. If indeed you can find it inside of you to believe me, I ask you to meet me in London in front of the St. Pauls Cathedral at II o'clock next Saturday night. Please try and bring as much money as you can, I'm sure that you'll be able to find some somewhere, maybe "borrow" off of Mother and Father. Do what you must, I trust you all.

I thank you all, and hope that you can help me,

Kind regards,

Winona.

I sealed it up and Ambrose sent it flying into the night, guaranteeing that it would reach one of them by the next morning. Now the plan had been set into action, all we had to do was wait.

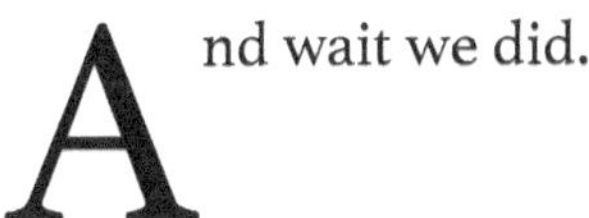

8

And wait we did.

But not for long. Saturday was only a week away and so, to pass the time, Ambrose took me sight-seeing around London. At night, of course. Ambrose had been living in London for about a year before I had come, so he knew his way around pretty well. We visited the clock tower and Big Ben – and we went right to the top of it, his magic lifting us up as high as we wanted to go.

When we got to the top, I saw the whole of London spread out before me. I grew very excited and turned around to tell Ambrose how amazing he was to bring me up. When I turned around he was right there in front of me. A few more inches and our lips would touch. My heart fluttered as he leaned in, our lips meeting. Heat flared up between us, sparks, whether they were a figment of my imagination or real, flew between us.

It was a wonderful first kiss. I don't believe it could've been any more perfect. It was long and sweet and seemed to go on forever, and his lips were oh so soft and tasted faintly of tea. Afterwards, he wrapped his arms around me and we held onto each other, breathing in each other's scents along with all the smells of night time London.

When Saturday finally came around, I became nervous. Ambrose could tell I was jitterish and did everything he could to calm me down, hugging me, kissing me, talking to me, but nothing he did worked.

Thoughts were racing through my mind. Would my friends come? What would they think of me when they saw me? Do I look different? I hadn't seen my reflection in a long time, so I went over to the broken mirror I had found but for some reason hadn't used.

For a second, I didn't recognise myself. Then I started to notice the similarities and the differences between my old self and now. My hair was still a lovely dark brown colour, although it had grown and now reached almost to my waist. My eyes, which had always been green, were somehow more intensely green. They had once been a lovely, forest green, but had changed to a sharp, beautiful and quite light green. My skin had always been pale, but was now nearly transparent, the blue of my veins slightly showing through.

I was beautiful. I hadn't been the best-looking woman in my social circle, but something in the transformation that I had gone through had sharpened my features and made me look more mature, and worldly. I wondered if Ambrose thought I was beautiful. I shook my head and stepped away from the mirror, back towards Ambrose.

Ambrose held out his arms and I went to him, snuggling myself right into the crook of his collarbone as if it had been made for me. He kissed my head and stroked my cheek, and then he whispered something, something I was almost certain that I had misheard.

He said it again and I knew that I hadn't. "I love you, Winona Hosking, more than I've ever loved anyone."

He flicked his fingers and all the candles in the room immediately lit up. It was beautiful.

I was shocked, too shocked almost, to say it back. But as I said it, I knew that I meant it. "I love you too, Ambrose."

I was in love?! Oh no, surely this would go horribly wrong.

We sat like that together, each thinking of what the other had just said. At least, I was until eventually, night came. Nervously, I got out of Ambrose's lap and turned around to pull him up. He had already leapt up and pulled me in for one last kiss before we left. As our lips met, the sparks that had started up the first night he kissed me, and hadn't stopped, again flew.

I had no idea if the feeling had anything to do with Ambrose's magic or not, but I liked it either way.

As we were walking towards the cathedral, hand in hand, I said, "Ambrose, what if they don't turn up? What if they believe every twisted thing that my father has surely told them? What if you're my only friend left?"

I was no longer able to keep my worries to myself.

He laughed, "Who wouldn't love you?"

He hugged me closer. It was a warm summer's evening, well, warm for London at least, and we only had overcoats on. I had long since sold my beautiful ball gown for scrap material. With all the blood stains, mud marks and tears in it, no one would have bought it. With the money from the scraps, I bought a few pairs of simple men's pants and some tunics. The men's clothing felt extremely weird on my body, and when I eventually saw my reflection, I didn't like the way the clothes hugged my body. But oh well, it was what had to be done. In my state, dresses were just no longer suitable.

We rounded the corner and St. Pauls Cathedral came into view. In front of it stood figures looking around nervously.

Were they nervous to see me? I wondered sadly.

As we approached them, they looked towards us from under their hooded cloaks. I recognised the faces of my three best friends, but whether I was still their best friend, I didn't know.

Agnes's face lit up when she saw me. Apparently, she thought nothing bad of me. The boys, however, were a bit more cautious. A smile slowly spread across Albus's face but Percival didn't warm to me at all. His actions made it clear that he was only here because he was supporting Agnes and Albus.

We exchanged polite hellos, although Agnes gave me a big hug – to my delight, and handed over an envelope that was almost bursting, along with a small sack of what looked like clothes and other provisions.

This meant a lot to me because most of it looked like Agnes's stuff, and she already had very little. As soon as we had finished the exchange, I was bombarded with questions.

"You're not really as bad as your father makes you out to be, are you?" Albus asked me, looking at Ambrose.

I realised that I hadn't introduced him to them yet. Oops. "Agnes, Albus, Percy, this is Ambrose Burnham, he's my um, friend. He's a witch. Ambrose, this is Agnes Ford, Albus Mottershed and Percival Henwood."

I didn't know what to call Ambrose. But he didn't seem bothered at all by that, and politely shook hands with them all in turn. Percy was rather hesitant, as if he thought he would catch a disease if he touched him.

I sighed. I didn't think I had three best friends anymore...

Once Albus found out that Ambrose was a witch, he immediately started a conversation with him, asking him about all sorts of magical beings or spells. How he knew so much already, I had no idea. Maybe he had found a couple of books in the library, or maybe it was something more...

But it was wonderful as it gave Agnes and me a chance to catch up.

"What's been happening back home?" I asked, needing to know something. "As you must have suspected, your father has spread the word that there was a demon in his household. Naturally, everyone in the village is too petrified to come out after dark, and all the apparent "witches" are selling items that are supposed to ward off demons. They're making a small fortune. I think they're the only ones benefiting from all this." She sighed. "I've missed you, Nona."

"I've missed you too, Agnes. You don't know what it's like to only be able to talk to a boy who's a couple of years older than you. He doesn't know what to talk about half the time."

We laughed and continued walking, checking to make sure that the boys were still behind us. Albus and Ambrose were deep in conversation, and Percival lagged behind them, clearly not wanting to join in on the reunion.

We walked and talked for quite a while, and it was lovely. I didn't realise how much I had missed my friends these past few weeks until I actually got to talk to them again. Albus, Agnes, Ambrose and I chatted happily as we strolled around night time London. Percival remained several paces behind us.

The look on his face said that he'd rather be anywhere but here.

Ambrose and I bid them farewell several

hours later. Percival really doesn't like me anymore, I thought sadly. Well it's his loss, the other, more devilish voice said.

I was surprised to find that I didn't care as much as I thought I would. It still hurt that he no longer thought of me as a friend, but two thirds of my friendship group still loved me even if I had become a blood-sucking demon thing, of the good sort though.

About an hour after they left, we set out on our own journey. With the envelope full of cash and clean clothes from Agnes, I felt a lot better about this adventure. Even though I thought most of it would be good, being with Ambrose, going on adventures and doing things I'd never done before, I had had some doubts. I had doubted whether my friends would come or not. They did. I worried whether we would have enough money. We definitely did. Would we run into trouble? Probably.

The last one I couldn't do anything about but, the first two I had done something about and I was proud of myself.

❖ 9 ❖

Soon we were on the train to Liverpool. Ambrose and I were curled up together in first class. The conductor hadn't believed that we had enough money for two first class tickets. He was judging by the way we looked, I suppose. But once we were settling in, I had to ask Ambrose a question that had been nagging me since he and I had first kissed.

"Ambrose?" I asked.

He looked down at me, fondly. "Yes?"

"Have you ever been in love? Before me?" He looked a little surprised when he heard that. He thought for a minute. "Hmm. I dunno, not exactly love, but I have had strong feelings for others. I am twenty years old, you know. I got around a bit. Never lasted long though. You?"

"One other, Marcellus. Not counting Zachariah, of course. He was my betrothed." I shuddered at the thought of having to spend the rest of my life with him. Ugh.

"What happened between you and Marcellus?" he asked, and my heart sank. Why he was interested in my earlier, almost non-existent love life, I have no idea. But this was one relationship I really didn't want to talk about.

"He died," I said softly. "He was my closest childhood friend, and one day, I thought I'd marry him."

"Oh," Ambrose said, almost as quiet. "How did he die?"

"He was killed by a bear in a hunting accident." I paused. "I loved him,"

Ambrose looked down, obviously saddened by the thought that I had loved someone else before him. "When was this?" he asked, maybe searching for answers that would make him feel better.

"When we were fifteen," I said.

"Am I just a rebound to make you feel better?" he asked, suddenly angry.

"No!" I cried. "Of course not!"

Although now that he said it, and even though I was pretty sure that I loved him, something small inside of me thought that maybe he was a rebound, just a little though.

Marcellus was a tragedy had happened when I was still a child. I was no longer the person that I used to be. I loved Ambrose, I thought. He was certainly not a rebound, I told myself – maybe it was to try and convince myself that it was true. I really just didn't know. I had a lot of mixed feelings and had only just been able to block them out.

Now the wall that I had built in my mind to keep out all the unwanted and painful memories was crumbling down, unleashing every wonderful and painful memory that I had had with Marcellus.

I pulled away from Ambrose and went to lie down on the other seat. Surprised, he opened his mouth to say something, but then closed it again. I could tell that he was angry and confused and didn't believe me when I said that our relationship wasn't just me trying to drown my feelings in another person's attention. God, I didn't even believe me. But I needed some alone time to think. He huffed and turned away from me, glaring out the window.

Three hours later, we pulled into the Liverpool train station. I could tell that Ambrose hadn't gotten over the little argument that we'd had earlier.

In fact, I think he'd gotten even more grouchy. Three hours was a long time for a horrible thought to be festering in his head, and I assumed that he'd begun to think up rather unlikely scenarios that would never happen. The mind could come up with all sorts of crazy ideas that spurred on your anger. That was what he was doing right now, I was sure of it.

Only later on did I find out how wrong I really was.

After we had exited the train carriage, Ambrose took me on a small tour of Liverpool while we waited for the sun to rise. Then we would have to retire to our inn. We didn't talk much, both of us were still rather moody from our fight on the train. So we avoided talking, just walking with our arms around each other.

As the sun started to rise and my skin started prickling, we headed back to find our inn. By the time we finally found it, my skin had started to sting and we ducked under cover just in time. As we entered through the doorway, I realised just how dingy the place was. We paid the innkeeper the measly amount of money that the inn was worth and headed up to our room.

When we got to our room I noticed that there was only one bed. I blushed and looked down. We'd discuss that later. I stepped further into the room and was disgusted by what I saw. Surely with all the money that we had could have paid for a nicer place?

Ambrose stepped up behind me and wrapped his arms around my waist. Resting his chin on the top of my head, he said, "I'm sorry it's not nicer. It's only for a couple of days."

He kissed the top of my head. I turned my head around and our lips met. All the anger and confusion that I'd had churned up inside of me disappeared and suddenly, I knew that I would be with this man for the rest of my life.

We spent the daytime resting and lounging about on the bed in our one tiny room. Ambrose's dark mood had returned, although this time it was a little less dark.

After he refused to come downstairs for a little while, I decided that I'd had enough. "Ambrose, why are you so upset that I've loved someone before you?" I asked.

He gave a short, sharp laugh. "You think that's why I'm upset? I wouldn't mind if you'd fallen in love with hundreds of men before me. Right now you love me, and I don't want that to change." His face was full of emotions – love, anger, sadness, concern. "No, that's not the reason I'm worried," he continued, "it's my fear that I'm going to lose you. That you'll find someone far better than me. Someone who has money, who has a good home. I'm not that man, and the thought of that terrifies me."

Wow, I had not expected that. And I knew for certain that this wasn't true. What he feared wouldn't happen. I wanted to spend

the rest of my life with this man.
So I told him.

"Ambrose Burnham, never in my life have I loved another the way I love you. I am going to spend the rest of your life by your side – if you'll allow it, of course. I am going to be with you when you are hurt and when you are strong. Whether you're sick or upset, I will be there to comfort you. I love you so much, Ambrose."

There were tears in my eyes, and more came when I realised that compared to the eternal life that I was going to have, Ambrose's lifetime was only going to be a small part of it. The thought of being away from him scared me beyond measure.

But we would sort that out when the time came because I could no longer think straight as I had been swept up into the most passionate kiss I had ever had. Our mouths moved in unison and his hands were threaded through my hair. I pulled his hair out of his ponytail ran my fingers through his silky blond waves.

We pulled apart and put our foreheads together, breathing in each other's scents.

Again, he smelt of warm peppermint tea and wood fire smoke. Those scents made me feel safe and warm. Even though we were in probably the dirtiest inn in Liverpool, right then, cuddling him on the half-broken bed in a room full of rat's holes and termite's nests was the only thing that I wanted in the world.

❖ IO ❖

When night fell, we set out to find the forest that Ambrose had spent his early childhood in, The Woods of Sortitus. We speedily made our way towards the edge of Liverpool, me running, and Ambrose keeping up by putting some form of magic spell on himself to be able to keep up. As the edge of the town came into view, and the trees rose up before us, Ambrose pulled me to a stop.

Confused, I looked up at him. "Why are we stopping?" I asked, pulling free and starting to head into the shadows of the trees.

He grabbed my arm again. "There's magic in the air," he said, acting strangely cautious for him.

"Well, it is apparently a magic forest, so yeah, there's magic," I replied. I didn't want to waste any time, and Ambrose was going rather slow.

"I know that there's supposed to be magic, but not this type. This is hostile and defensive magic. I don't like this at all."

I sighed. It looked like we were going to be doing this his way.

Quietly, Ambrose ventured into the forest with me not far behind him. Coming from a wealthy family, and being a woman, I wasn't so practiced in stepping without making any noises, despite all my time in the woods. Percy had always complained about my loud footfalls, claiming that they scared away all the prey. I smiled at those memories, even though I knew that I would not be able make any new memories with him.

Ambrose stopped suddenly and I just avoided crashing into him, my nose coming to a stop at the base of his neck. Again, why was he so tall, and I so short?!

"What is it?" I whispered, these woods were starting to give me the creeps and I was eager to find his cabin.

"Someone's watching us," he whispered

back.

Okay, now I really wanted to get out of here.

"How do you know?" I asked, fighting hard to keep the fear out of my voice.

He paused for a second, and turned to look behind me. I turned around to see what he was looking at. Nothing.

"I can feel it," he said, as he turned back to me. His voice had gone down a notch, and I could barely hear him now.

He froze. "There!"

I whipped around and heard a rustle of leaves behind me. I looked down and just saw a glimpse of white before whatever it was disappeared into the bushes.

Ambrose leapt into action, holding his hands out in front of him, "VENI!" he shouted, and a little white figure with four legs and the torso of a boy streaked towards us, coming to a standstill in front of us.

I suspected that that was Ambrose's doing, as the boy was struggling to move, but couldn't. He seemed to be a centaur, only much, much smaller. Even a child centaur wouldn't be this small. It was as if he was a Shetland centaur, if those existed… My thoughts were cut short, and I was brought back to the present.

Ambrose was shouting at him and the poor thing looked ready to break down. "Who are you? What are you doing here? Where's the leading witch?" his voice slowly rose higher and higher, and I feared that the whole forest would hear us.

"Ambrose! Stop it, you're scaring him half to death!" I stepped in front of Ambrose, shielding the boy from his deathly gaze.

"What are doing?" he asked, the anger slowing leaking from his voice.

"Look at him!" I demanded.

Ambrose looked around me at the boy who was indeed cowering behind me, looking as if he might faint from fright.

Ambrose's gaze softened.

"He's just a boy," I calmly told him, "leave

him be."

Ambrose advanced on the young centaur, an apologetic look on his face. He stopped walking towards him. "If this centaur is only a child, why is it that he has a beard?"

I looked at him, indeed before, in my rush to save him from a heart attack, I had failed to notice that he had a scraggly little beard growing out of his chin. The little centaur puffed out his small chest, and rose to his entire 8 hands and exclaimed, "How very rude of you! I am Titus Evander of the Sortitus Clan and I am still growing!"

Ambrose and I exchanged glances. "Sortitus Clan? What's that?" Ambrose asked.

I wondered if he was thinking what I was. Is this the Clan we've been looking for?

Titus Evander answered Ambrose's question almost immediately, it obviously hadn't crossed his mind that he was giving information to outsiders. "The Sortitus Clan is the power of this forest," he said proudly. "Our leader is the all-powerful witch Parthena Grenhadyn."

I looked over at Ambrose and, by the expression on his face, I could gather that this witch Parthena Grenhadyn was indeed who we were looking for.

The little centaur continued, unaware of our expressions. "And we have won many wars. But that was a long time ago. This forest is the heart of peace and prosperity, everyone gets along here, except for the tree trolls, of course. They are rather grumpy."

He went on and on about the forest, giving us none of the information that we needed.

Eventually, I had to cut in. "Now Titus, that's all very interesting. But we've heard enough for now. Could you take us to Parthena Grenhadyn?"

This time he hesitated, probably thinking about the consequences of taking outsiders into the heart of his world. Eventually, he came to a decision. "All right," he said, "but on one condition."

"What is it?" I asked, eager to meet this Parthena.

"I want that lovely necklace that you have

around your neck."

I looked down. I had forgotten about my necklace. It had a bright red ruby in the middle of it with gold weaved around the edges. It had been a gift from my grandmother, and I didn't want to give it up. But solemnly, I unclasped the necklace and dropped it into his palm. There was a scar that ran all the way up his arm and around his neck.

What happened there? I wondered.

Satisfied with my sacrifice, Titus set off into the woods at a brisk pace. I had no trouble keeping up with him, but after about twenty minutes, Ambrose started to lag behind.

"STOP!" I called out, and Titus skidded and narrowly missed a log that was lying across the almost non-existent path.

Something about him made me wonder if he was an outsider himself. He seemed rather unsure of where he was going, and eager to have an excuse to get inside the group. If we ever got there. Ambrose came up behind us, puffing. His cheeks were red and he had scratches all over his face and hands. Being human, his eyes weren't as adjusted to the dark as mine were. Sweat had begun to drip down his face, and I wrinkled my nose at the strong smell.

The others looked at me weirdly. *Oh right, vampire senses. Ugh.* Ambrose blushed and wiped his face with the front of his shirt. *We really need to wash before we meet this witch.* "Titus, is there a stream nearby where we can wash?"

"Yeah, we should cross one in about twenty minutes."

We set off again, and sure enough, despite my many doubts, we came across a bubbling stream. The reflection of the moon rippled across the surface, and the surrounding trees were bleached of all colour, giving the area a surreal, magic look. The whole scene gave me a strange sense of déjà vu.

I went behind a large rock and stripped down to my underclothes. Undressing is a lot easier when you're a boy, I decided. I lowered myself into the icy water, sucking in air sharply through my teeth. Once I had adjusted to the temperature of the water, I fully submerged myself. It was nowhere near as lovely as the hot baths that I was used to having, but the water was refreshing and it was the first "bath" I'd had in a long while.

I scrubbed our clothes and lay them out to dry on the rock. It was still dark, but the air was warming up, telling me that the sun would soon start rising. We find a little nook in the rocks that was just big enough for the three of us to get comfy. I hadn't expected Titus to stay with us once I told him about my "sickness" but he didn't seem bothered at all and left to find some grass to munch on.

Once he had left, Ambrose and I curled up in a corner. Just as I was drifting off to sleep, Ambrose spoke.
"What if there was a way for you to walk around in sunlight?" he asked, suddenly.

I was wide awake. I wished for nothing more than to be able to walk in the sunlight again. "How?" I asked.

"Well, I've heard of an enchantment that can charm an object into doing something that you want. Say that you wanted wealth, you can enchant a ring or something, and then, when you wear it, wealth will come almost instantly. It's very tricky though, only a very powerful witch could do it."

My heart sunk. I didn't think that, despite his magical abilities, Ambrose was any- where near powerful enough to do an en- chantment of that size, and I doubted that Parthena would do us this favour for noth- ing in return.

❖ **II** ❖

As the sun started to sink below the horizon and I could leave the shadows of the cave with only a slight tingle on my skin, Ambrose, Titus and I set out again. Titus was sure that we were getting close, only about two more hours of walking.

For most of our walk, Titus was informing us of stuff that we had no interest in knowing. "And my mother was short as well, but my father was tall. So I'm still growing!" He went on, and on, and on.

He really is like a child with a beard... I thought.

After about an hour, Ambrose had had enough, and frankly, so had I. "That's *enough* centaur, we've heard enough," he said, sternly.

The little centaur huffed and crossed his

arms, he beat his hooves down hard as he stomped a few feet in front of us.

This gave Ambrose and I some privacy to talk. "Do you think he knows where he's going?" I asked, wrapping my arm around his waist.

"Not in the slightest, but he's our best chance of finding Parthena. And, who knows, maybe he'll accidentally stumble across a path or a tree that he recognises."

I laughed, he smiled and looked up. The moon was nearly at its peak, and it cast a beautiful light over the scenery. I sighed, what I would give to be able to walk in the sunlight, and I suspected that Ambrose was getting sick of being confined to the shadows.

Another hour passed, and I felt inclined to ask the question that Ambrose and I had both been wondering. "Are we lost?"

Titus halted, a strange look on his face. "N-no- o- no," he stammered, sounding more like a "horse" than he had yet. He continued walking.

"Stop," I said, my voice firm.

The centaur stopped and turned around, his face contorted into what looked like a mix of determination, fear, guilt, and just a touch of anger. Although he tried to smother it, I knew that something was wrong.

And as if like clockwork, just as I thought it, everything descended into chaos.

Men in black and grey uniforms and slung with all kinds of weapons, rifles, bows, hatchets, anything that could potentially kill, burst out of the bushes and fell out of the trees, surrounding us.

Titus whinnied and reared onto his tiny back legs. He only just made it to the top of my head. His eyes widened, and I saw just how wild he really was. I turned to Ambrose, my face starting to fill with fear, but he had already flung into action, his palms towards the men, jets of light ere bursting through them and knocking the men back. But for every man that he incapacitated, two filled his place.

I kicked into gear, and swung left and right, not knowing who I was hitting. I let my fangs out, and for the first time since my eighteenth birthday, I let out the monster that was inside me, dying to get out. I forced my way through the crowd, sinking my teeth into anyone who got too close. I didn't feel any mercy at this point. But I knew that afterwards, I would probably feel shameful and regret what I had done.

Kicking and biting, I made my way to where Ambrose was getting slowly overwhelmed by the onslaught of men. I joined him, blood dripping down my face, and back to back we fought off anyone that came near us. Ambrose had only a second to look at me before he had been drawn back into the chaos, but the look on his face as he saw me, blood streaming out of my mouth and onto my shirt, had chilled me.

It had been a mix of awe, love, disgust, but most of all, fear.

It upset me. The man I loved was afraid of me, of what I could do. I would never forgive myself if I lost control and hurt him, it would have been disastrous. I pulled myself back into the fight, surprised that I could think and fight at the same time.

We fought for a long time. They just kept coming and coming. I wondered where Titus had gotten to. *Had he led us into a trap?* I wondered, and anger flooded through me, urging me to fight harder.

I looked around, my legs and arms flailing about in all kinds of defensive and offensive manoeuvres. Just as I had decided that this *had* been Titus' doing, I spotted a hoof. Following the hoof I saw Titus, unconscious and blood streaming out of a gash on his head. I hoped that he was alright. I forced myself to focus on the task at hand.

A man in his forties with greying hair came at me, a pitchfork in his left hand and a spade in his right, he took a swing at me and wobbled slightly. I sunk my teeth into his neck deep enough to knock him out. Whoever these guys were, they weren't built for fighting. I had managed to stop myself from killing anybody yet, by sinking my fangs in just deep enough that they fall unconscious.

Someone grabbed me from behind and I lashed out. My fist connected with his face and I whirled around, he let go of me and I took a good look at him while he was recovering. I stopped, utterly shocked. I could only just stop my jaw from dropping open.

In front of me, in a black and grey uniform and holding a rifle, blood dripping from his nose, was Percy.

Too shocked to move, I stood as Percy rushed at me and shot me through the chest, once, twice, three times. I barely felt it. I turned to look for Ambrose and, as if in slow motion, I saw him fall to the ground, blood streaming from three points in his chest.

"AMBROSE!" I screamed.

I started to rush towards him, but something hit my head, and I descended into darkness.

❖ 12 ❖

I woke up in a darkness that not even my vampire eyes could adjust to. My hands were tied and there was a strange smell in the air. The first thought that came to my head was Ambrose, falling to the ground, hit by the three bullets that had passed right through me and into him. I felt around in the dark for my chest and found that it was sticky with blood. I felt like anyone would if they'd had three bullets pass right through them. The pain was almost intolerable.

I bit my lip to stop myself from crying out. I will not show weakness! As hard as I tried to stop myself, I felt myself getting drawn back into the darkness.

I was jolted awake by the wheels of a carriage going over rocky ground. I looked at my surroundings. I was in a bare carriage. Sunlight was pouring into the carriage and I was forced to push myself into a corner, my feet barely avoiding being singed. My hands were still bound behind my back, and I was too drained to be able to get out of the metal cuffs that surrounded my wrists.

Why am I so tired? I never get tired... I felt so, so tired.

For the third time, I woke. The sun had started setting, and the door to my carriage was being unlocked. The door opened and the little sunlight left filled the carriage and my skin started stinging. A shadow crossed the doorway and l looked up. My grandfather stood there. I supposed I should have known that he wasn't going to give up after just one failed attempt at killing me.

He looked down on me. "Ahhh, Winona dear. How are you? I would say that you look well, had the devil not possessed you."

I scowled at him and he laughed. He pulled something out of his pocket, a needle with a reddish colour liquid in it. Too bright to be blood, it was almost as if...

"Rowan berries. *Of course,*" I muttered to myself. It made sense that the berries of the tree that could kill me would do something and I suspected that that was what was making me so weak.

He leaned down with the needle, and struggle as I did, I could not dodge the needle's pointy edge. A sharp prick and my body was filled with an icy cold feeling. Almost immediately my eyes began to droop. I fought to keep them open but found that it was impossible. As my vision blurred, the last thing I saw was my grandfather's grinning face, imprinted on the back of my eyelids.

Once again, I awoke. I wondered how many more times I would be drugged and woken.

I looked at my surroundings and gasped. I was in a clearing of trees. Whether I was still in The Woods of Sortitus, I didn't know. I was on a platform about ten feet off the ground, my hands were tied around the back of the pole.

Surely this wasn't good. I looked around some more and shouted for help but it was no good. Wherever I was, there was no one willing or in earshot to help. I spotted movement over at the far edge of the clearing.

Two men had just entered. One around my

age, and the other was in his seventies. It was Percy and my grandfather, Isaiah.

Percy's betrayal hit me hard. He had made it very clear that he didn't want anything to do with me, but to work with my grandfather? That was a whole new level of betrayal.

Something glinted in my grandfather's hand. *The stake*, I realised. Suddenly, it became all too real. *I am going to die.* I started shaking, I wasn't ready to die! Even without my vampire eternity, I was young and had my whole life ahead of me.

As the sky brightened, my skin started tingling and I started panicking. I tried to slow my breathing. Freaking out was not going to help my situation. I calmed my breathing and started to think of a way out. I am *the vampire, I am strong and invincible.*

But under the influence of Rowan juice, I was weak and vulnerable. In a few short hours, the sun would fully rise and I would crumble to before the sun sank below the horizon. That was something I had to stop at all costs.

The sky was turning a deep red, orange colour. In any other circumstance I would have found it beautiful. But now, as my torturer rose further into the sky, I could think of nothing but how to escape.

The shadow of the trees around me were receding, and soon, I would be in direct sunlight, burning until I could no longer take it, begging to be killed.

I'm was on fire. My face, my neck, my arms, my legs burned with such intensity that I started screaming. I'd never screamed so loud before. Birds flew from the trees and the men below covered their ears, but still they grinned up at me. Tears streamed down my face.

Far below me, my grandfather was grinning maliciously from ear to ear, his eyes hard and cold and showing no mercy. I was a *thing* that needed to be extinguished, he needed to rid the world of me.

Percy, on the other hand, was not grinning. He was not smiling at all. I looked into his eyes and I saw my pain and anguish reflected back at me. *He regrets this.* I thought to myself, trying to distract myself from the pain. I imagined Isaiah, burning in the depths of the hell he would so surely go to. I imagined him screaming, just as I am, as his flesh burnt away, just as mine had. I imagined Percy, plagued by the guilt of what he had done, taking his own life. I could hear the gunshot going through his hollow skull, exploding his rather small excuse for a brain. And then, I imagined Ambrose. Wounded somewhere, all alone. Possibly dead. And, despite my burning situation, an icy wave of fear shot through me at the thought of living forever without Ambrose.

The pain was like thousands of red-hot knives stabbing me and scraping up and down my body. I had never felt anything so agonising. I hoped I would never feel anything so agonising again.

I would love to say that I stood strong while I was on that post. But I didn't. I screamed and at various points I fainted from the pain. And then, when grandfather *finally* pulled out the stake and climbed up the ladder to where I was tied, I was ready to die.

But instead of stabbing me with the stake, he began to scrape and jab the point of it up and down my face, leaving fiery trails. I screamed and I shouted, my face wet with tears.

"Why are you doing this, you monster?" I mustered up the strength to spit in his face.

He laughed. "Oh, Winona. When will you learn? It's not that easy." He spat back at me. "I can't have you going around telling people what I've done. It's bad for business." A malicious grin spread across his face. He moved the stake down my face and onto my arms. I struggled, but I was still weakened by the poison coursing through my bloodstream.

Eventually he got bored with tormenting me himself and left me to the sun.

I came to with a jerk. I didn't realise that I had passed out again. Whether it was the pain or the poison, I did not know. Sagging at my post, I noticed that the thick ropes tying me so tight to the pole were not cutting into my body anymore. I wriggled around, experimenting with what I could do to make them looser. This was good.

It had taken several agonizing hours for the effects of the Rowan berry juice to start wearing off. My flesh had started to blister away, but despite this I felt stronger – and even though my skin was sizzling and burning, I no longer wanted to die. I wanted to get out of here.

Again, I thought of Ambrose, somewhere out there with three bullets embedded in his body that were meant for me. Desperate, I wriggled a bit more, and found that the ropes were now loose enough for me to pull free. I dropped to the ground, wary of the witch-hunter who was still guarding me. When he saw me jump down he came at me with a very sharp-looking blade. I swerved to avoid him and elbowed him between the shoulder blades. He crumpled to the ground and I raced away into the forest, determined to find the boy I loved.

❖ 13 ❖

I raced through the forest. I don't know how but I felt as if I had a thread pulling me towards something. I had learned that wondering would get me nowhere, so I just decided to follow the feeling, to pretend that everything was normal.

I ran for what seemed like hours, but I never tired. My love for Ambrose still glowed strong, and I pushed myself faster. I raced past a rock wall. Small caves were dotted around, probably safe houses for the magical beings of this wonderful forest.

I heard a groan and skidded to a stop. The magical string pulling me ever on had disappeared.

"Ambrose?!" I called out.

I heard another groan and someone wheezing. I followed the sound to a cave about fifty feet away. I entered the cave and immediately dropped to the floor.

Ambrose and Titus were lying on the floor, blood pooling around them.

I take back what I said about burning under the sun at the stake. That *wasn't* the most agonising thing I'd ever felt. Seeing Ambrose like this – mangled, bloody and infected, so close to dying? This was much, much worse.

I have to do something! I thought. I was starting to panic. I took some deep breaths and cleared the panicky thoughts crowding my head. I knelt beside Ambrose. He tried to lift his head, causing him to cry out in pain. More blood gushed out of his wounds. *What do I do?!* I had no medical training. I could barely bandage a cut. *No, that was* before *I became a vampire. I've done so much since. I can do this.*

I took another deep breath and pulled Ambrose into a sitting position so he was leaning against the cave wall. I had a better view of what I was working with now. But that caused me to take a sharp breath. What I saw was not good. His shirt had been ripped and his bare stomach underneath was shiny and red. His stomach and chest were hot to touch. I knew enough to know that his wounds were becoming infected.

I ripped what was left of his shirt off his chest and worked in a trance-like state. Ambrose came to enough to quietly instruct me. If I didn't have extreme hearing, I doubt I would have been able to hear him, he was so weak. I went outside and found a leaf big and strong enough to hold water. I then raced to the stream, aware that Ambrose was dying but not able to go any faster. I sponged off as much of the blood as possible and ripped up my shirt for bandages. There was moss on the rocks outside the cave entrance and Ambrose guided me as I used the moss for padding and wrapped bits of my tattered shirt around his torso. Once Ambrose was in a more stable condition, I moved over to assess Titus.

Titus had a large gash on his forehead that looked slightly infected, and his left hind leg was bent at an odd angle. *Broken.* I treated his head with the remainder of my shirt strips and some more moss, wrapping them around his small head. Then I moved onto his leg. It didn't look good. His hoof was lifted up and I could see the white of his bone starting to poke out. I checked to see if he was still passed out. He was. *Thank god, I don't know how much more pain his little body can take*, I thought to myself.

Once again, I calmed my breathing and readied myself. CRACK! I broke his leg all the way.

Titus woke up with a shout. "What are you doing to me?!"

He shrieked even louder when he saw his leg. It took a few seconds for the shock to wear off and the pain to kick in. Then he shrieked some more while I set the bone again with a splint.

It broke my heart to hear Titus crying. It even woke Ambrose, and probably scared off any nearby animals. Tears streaming down his small face, Titus asked what happened. "Where did you go?" He sobbed.

I was not sure if he was sobbing because I had gone, or because of his leg.

I explained all about my grandfather. I told him everything from the start. How my grandfather had selfishly doomed the next girl born in the family to a life cursed with bad luck. His eyes widened when I told him of Percy's betrayal and how the witch who cursed me had lost control of the curse, which is how it had spiralled and turned me into what I was now.

More tears streamed down his dear face as I told him about how the curse was too strong for the witch to hold onto and she had to let it run wild.

Movement from Ambrose's corner made me pause and look over. He had passed out shortly after I had finished with him, and had just come to. He struggled to push himself upright. I rushed over to help him, moving him away from the wall and putting his head on my shoulder.

Fear coursed through me, chilling me. His head was sweltering and beads of sweat were dripping down his face. *Fever. Oh no, this isn't good. A fever means that his wounds are infected.*

He started to say something that even I could not hear. I put my ear to his mouth. "I'm... dy-dying...my darling," he shivered.

Although his forehead was the temperature of a boiled kettle, he was shaking with cold.

I would not accept it, "*No*," I said firmly. "I'm not letting you die. I'm not letting you go." Tears started to fall down my face. *I would not* let him die because of me.

He gave a sad little laugh. "I'm *infected* Win. My body's shutting down. I won't make it to the morning."

"No, no, no! There's got to be something I can do."

"It's okay," he whispered. "In my short life-time, I had the pleasure of meeting you, going on this adventure, falling in love with you. It's all been worth it." His voice was getting quieter and quieter, his eyes becoming more and more vacant.

"NO!" I shouted.

This couldn't be happening. In a desperate attempt to save him, I remembered something that Letitia had said:

You have the power to bring back the dying. All it takes is a small bite.

No, I thought to myself. I couldn't put this burden on him. He would rather die. A selfish voice at the back of my head started talking. *But think about it*, the voice hissed, *you could be together eternally…*

My two sides warred with each other, and slowly, slowly, Ambrose slipped further and further away from me.

I gave in to my selfish voice. I couldn't stand the thought of living in a world without him. I leant down to his neck. I could hear his heartbeat, slower and slower until I could barely hear it. I opened my mouth and sank my fangs into the side of his neck, drinking his blood.

Then I fell into a desolate heap and sobbed.

A little while later, he lurched upwards. His back bent in an unhuman way, and then he fell unconscious again.

What have I done?!

I put my ear beside his mouth to check if he was breathing. He wasn't. I fell back in agony. I'd killed him. Ambrose was dead and it was my fault. Titus dragged his broken body over to me and we held each other and cried. I cried and I cried. I had never been so anguished in my life.

❖ 14 ❖

Ambrose bolted upright beside me. Titus, who had fallen asleep with his leg curled up beside me, yelped in fright. My mouth fell open. What was going on? Ambrose was dead, I'd seen the life drain away from him as the infection took over.

But no, here he was, looking bright and healthy. I had bitten him and it had worked. That was the only possible answer. Before he could say anything, I bombarded him with a hug. He swept me up and pressed his lips to mine. He was different, but the same. He still smelt and tasted like Ambrose, tea leaves and magic, but his skin was paler and more translucent, like mine.

For a second, I worried that he would hate me for what I had done to him. I'd turned him into a monster like me.

"I could never hate you, Win," he said. His voice was musical and filled my heart with joy.

"Did I say that out loud?" I asked, surprised. Apparently, I tended to say things aloud without realising.

He paused. "No, no I don't think so…" A thoughtful expression fell upon his face. "Think something," he said. "Anything."

Slightly confused, I thought, *I love you Ambrose Burnham. And thinking that you were dead nearly killed me.*

Ambrose smiled. "I can read your mind. That will be useful." He mused. "I've heard of this happening. But I only thought it happened when you got transformed…"

As per usual, I had no clue whatsoever as to what he was talking about. I looked to him for an explanation and he paused to explain.

"Sometimes, if a mortal's will is strong and their heart is pure enough, they can be transformed from a mere mortal into a powerful witch. In extreme and rare cases, they have been known to acquire extra powers, such as mind reading. Like me. Others are more powerful – they are immortal, resistant to fire, invisible and so on." He paused to look at me, making sure that I was taking all of this in and then continued. "But I never thought that it could happen with other transformations. We have so much to learn!"

A big smile appeared on his face. His excitement made me happy.

"I love you too," he whispered, and he swept me up into another, longer kiss that wrapped me up in the moment.

In that moment, I forgot about that man trying to kill me. I forgot that he used to be part of my family. I forgot that all I could eat or drink was the blood of a living thing. All I knew was that I wanted to spend the rest of eternity with this wonderful boy.

And I would.

Acknowledgments

First off, I would like to give a huge thank you to my auntie, Hilary. Thank you so much for all the help, ideas and encouragement that you've given me. You inspire me. Thank you to my Mum and Dad, for not being biased and giving me honest answers and good advice. Thanks to my two amazing school guardians, Tony and April, for making this happen – if it wasn't for you guys, I probably wouldn't have gotten the chance to write a book at this age. And lastly, thank you to my friends for helping me and being honest about parts of the book that they did and didn't like; you know who you are.

About the Author

My name is Noni Munro-Rogers. I wrote this book. Now, I know you're all wondering the same thing - what's this thirteen-year-old doing, thinking she can write. Believe me, I'm thinking it too.

I didn't expect this book to become *an actual book*. I was doing it for a school assignment, I was planning on printing out one copy and then handing it in. And then, lo & behold it became an actual thing.

So here it is. Who knows, maybe I'll write more and eventually become an author.

9 780648 341802